Daniel Torres

TOM

VIKING

English-language adaption by Julie Simmons-Lynch.

The artwork was done in black ink and watercolor.

VIKING
Published by the Penguin Group
Penguin Books USA Inc., 375 Hudson Street, New York, New York 10014, U.S.A.
Penguin Books Ltd, 27 Wrights Lane, London W8 5TZ, England
Penguin Books Australia Ltd, Ringwood, Victoria, Australia
Penguin Books Canada Ltd, 10 Alcorn Avenue, Toronto, Ontario, Canada M4V 3B2
Penguin Books (N.Z.) Ltd, 182–190 Wairau Road, Auckland 10, New Zealand

Penguin Books Ltd, Registered Offices: Harmondsworth, Middlesex, England

First published in Spain by Norma Editorial, 1995
First published in the United States of America by Viking,
a division of Penguin Books USA Inc., 1996
First published in Great Britain by Penguin Books Ltd, 1996

1 3 5 7 9 10 8 6 4 2

Copyright © Daniel Torres, 1995
English-language translation copyright © Penguin Books USA Inc., 1996
All rights reserved
Library of Congress Catalog Card Number: 95-61266
ISBN 0-670-86665-2
Printed in Spain
Set in Futura

This is Tom. He loves to travel. Most people travel by car, train, plane, or even on a bike, but not Tom. *He* prefers to travel on his island. He can steer himself quite nicely with his tail.

One day, Tom felt like going somewhere. So he packed a toothbrush and a change of socks, and headed out for parts unknown.

On and on he sailed, until finally he came to a port where he saw a gigantic woman holding up a very large flashlight.

She looked friendly, so when Tom was close enough he climbed up and introduced himself. Then something big and shiny and beautiful caught his eye. It was a steamship, the grandest ship he had ever seen. Tom said goodbye to his new friend and followed the steamship toward land.

The steamship docked amidst a blizzard of flags and confetti. How nice to be welcomed with a party!

Tom saw that the steamship passengers were getting off the ship and heading onto dry land, so he climbed off his island and did the same. But there wasn't much of a welcome party *here*. In fact, most people ignored Tom.

Then a man dressed in blue said to Tom, "Move it, buddy! You're in a no-standing zone."

Tom thought it might be a good time to continue exploring this strange new place.

He found a big park filled with lakes and meadows and trees (and a carousel he almost tripped over). And leaves, too . . . leaves that tickled his nose!

ACHOOO! ACHOOO! Tom's sneeze made it look just like autumn.

Too bad it was only May.

Soon it was lunchtime. Being a courteous sort, Tom even brought his own fork.

But no matter how politely Tom asked for a bite of this or a morsel of that, he was ignored. Well, not exactly ignored. People threw things at him, but nothing he could eat.

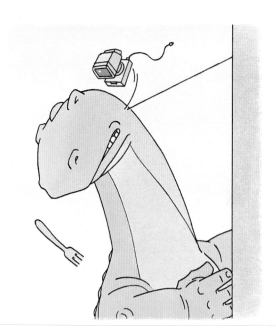

Things continued like that all day. Finally, as darkness fell, Tom found a place that reminded him of his little island. He climbed up there to spend the night.

Tom sat atop his new island and looked around him, feeling a little lonely.

Tomorrow would be a better day.

The next morning, Tom woke up, stretched, and brushed his teeth. Then he watched what the people in the streets were doing. How could he fit in?

Tom noticed that people generally had somewhere to go, and were hurrying every which way to get there. Then Tom realized: they all had jobs. Maybe he needed one too.

But Tom found all too quickly that he wasn't cut out to be an elevator man.

. . . Or a firefighter, a policeman, or a chef.

Tom also discovered that driving a train wasn't exactly like steering his little island!

But Tom didn't give up. He was big and strong—maybe helping to build a skyscraper would be the right job for him.

Of course, sometimes it's better not to do *everything* all at once!

Tom was not asked to come back the next day.

Poor Tom! He wondered if his little island felt as lonely as *he* did.

The next morning, a boy named Billy was walking to school, when he noticed that there were big round dots on the sidewalk. Billy couldn't help thinking that they reminded him of dinosaur tracks.

Billy decided to follow the big dots to see where they led.

Blue dot . . . yellow dot . . . red dot . . . Dot after dot, until finally Billy found himself on the observation deck of a very tall building. "Wow!" Billy shouted. "A dinosaur right here in New York City!"

Tom didn't know what a dinosaur was, but he did know he had finally found a friend.

"Would you like to come over to my apartment and play?" Billy asked Tom.

Of course Tom said yes!

When they reached Billy's home, Billy shouted, "Hi Dad! Can the dinosaur come and live with us?"

His father, a very important art critic, was busy writing down terrible things about a painting he had just seen. "Well, what does the dinosaur do?" he replied absentmindedly.

"He's an artist," Billy shouted back. "An *excellent* artist!"

"An artist?" repeated his father. He leaned out the window and saw how Tom's feet, still wet with paint, had adorned the city. "Heavens," his father exclaimed. "He could be the next Pigasso or Andy Warthog!"

"An artistic dino!" Billy's father went on excitedly. "This could be the start of Prehistoric Pop Art!"

Prehistoric Pop Art sounded important, but as long as Tom could stay, that's all Billy and Tom cared about.

Billy's father began making phone calls. First he called the hardware store to order 500 gallons of paint. Then he called all the art journals to tell them that he had just discovered a major new artist.

Almost before you could say "Brontosaurus blitz," Tom had covered the Big Apple with paint—and every newspaper, magazine, and TV show had covered Tom. He was named Artist of the Year.

How strange it all was! One minute nobody seemed to want him, and the next nobody could do without him. Tom couldn't make a move without a crowd following and cheering him on.

Looking at Tom, you might have thought that he had everything. But Tom was finding that being famous had its drawbacks.

The problem was, he had to be famous all day long. He was so busy giving interviews, autographing T-shirts, and going to glamorous parties that there wasn't much time to spend with Billy. And there weren't many places they could go where they weren't mobbed by Tom's fans. It's hard to hide a dinosaur in New York City!

Soon they ran out of hiding places, and Billy noticed that more and more, Tom was looking longingly out to sea. So finally Billy placed his freckled cheek on Tom's nose and told him, "I know you're not happy here, and you're just staying on because of me." Billy gave a big sniff and went on bravely, "But I can't be happy if you're not happy, and I think it's time you continued on your travels."

"I'll miss you tons, Tom," Billy said sadly.

Tom blinked back tears but didn't cry since he knew they didn't make tissues big enough for his nose. He and Billy started packing, and by sunset, Tom was on his way.

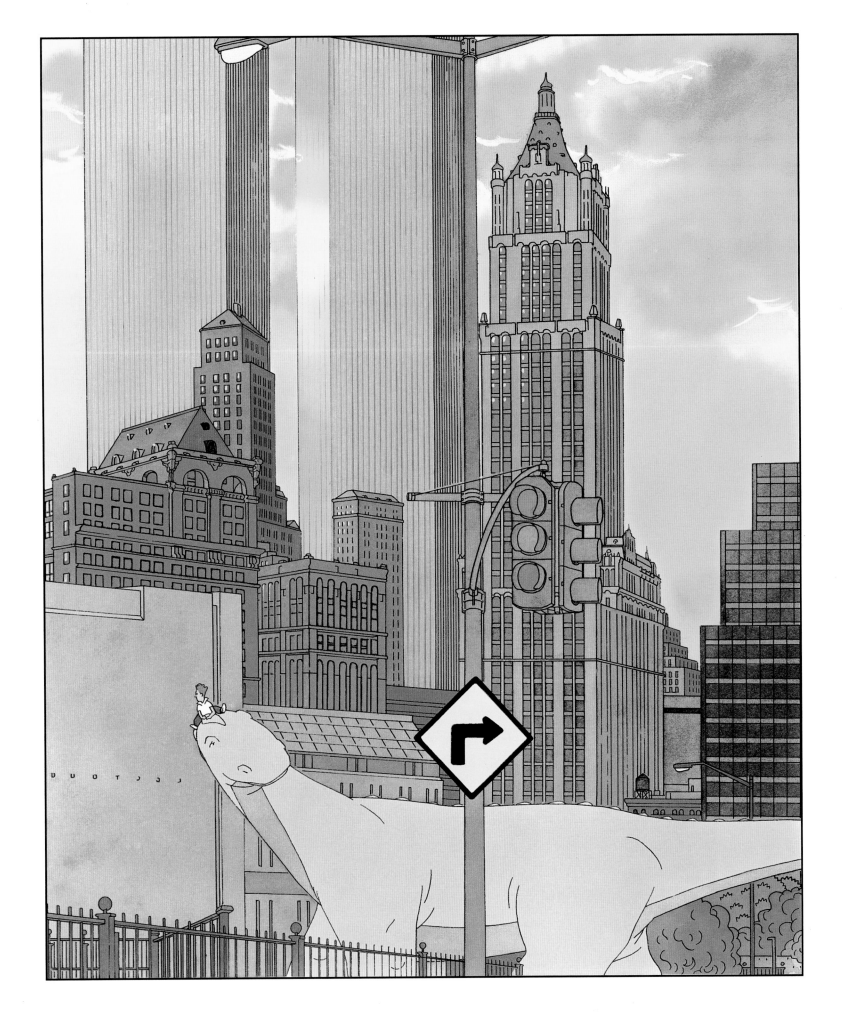

Billy thinks of Tom every day. His father, who took Tom's departure surprisingly well (secretly he was relieved to go back to his quiet life), gave Billy a pet frog. While having a frog isn't quite like having a dinosaur, at least he doesn't cause the same commotion wherever he goes. (Except for the time he got loose in the girls' locker room at school, but that's another story.)

And Tom? Well, he's still on the move. Who knows, he might even come to your town—so keep an eye out for him. He's a big fellow, artistic, friendly . . . and very conscientious about brushing his teeth. But when he rinses, watch out!